GOD'S ETERNAL PLAN

WATCHMAN NEE

Living Stream Ministry
Anaheim, California • www.lsm.org

© 1993 Living Stream Ministry

All rights reserved. No part of this work may be reproduced or transmitted in any form or by any means—graphic, electronic, or mechanical, including photocopying, recording, or information storage and retrieval systems—without written permission from the publisher.

West African Edition, 2,000 copies. September 2002

This edition may be sold in West Africa only.

ISBN 0-7363-0627-7

Distributed in West Africa by
Ghana Gospel Book Room
P.O. Box CE 12375
Tema, Ghana

Published by

Living Stream Ministry
2431 W. La Palma Ave., Anaheim, CA 92801 U.S.A.
P.O. Box 2121, Anaheim, CA 92814 U.S.A.

Printed in Nigeria

CONTENTS

Title	Page
Foreword	5
1 Introduction	7
2 The Prayer that Expresses God's Will	11
3 What Is God's Eternal Will	19
4 The Son of God and the Christ	21
5 The Rebellion of the Angels	25
6 God's Purpose in Creating Man	31
7 The Fall of Man	37
8 The Work of Christ	41
9 The Organization, Goal, and Methods of Satan's Kingdom	47
10 The Position and Responsibility of the Church	53

FOREWORD

The book contains a series of ten messages from a conference given by Watchman Nee. While the location and date of the conference are unknown, it was most likely conducted in Shanghai in 1939. The main subject of the conference was God's eternal plan. The messages explain the two eternities and the meaning of God's eternal plan. They expound the Lord's prayer and its relationship to God's eternal plan. They point out Christ the Son of God and His place in God's eternal plan. They cover the origin of Satan, the purpose of the creation of man and his fall, and the work of Christ in fulfilling God's eternal plan. They expose Satan's organization and methods in frustrating God's eternal plan, and they conclude by revealing the position and responsibility of the church in God's eternal plan.

Chapter One

INTRODUCTION

Scripture Reading: Eph. 3:11; 1:9, 11

WHAT ETERNITY IS

God has an eternal plan in eternity. This plan is made according to His will. In order to know God's eternal plan, we first must know what eternity is. The Bible shows us that eternity has two parts. We can call them the *first eternity* and the *second eternity* (see diagram):

```
The first eternity ─┬─ Heavens ─┬─ The second eternity
                    └─ Earth ───┘
```

The First Eternity

The *beginning* in John 1:1 is the beginning of the Word. We do not know the time of the beginning of the Word. The beginning of the Word is the eternity without a beginning. This is the first eternity. (The beginning of the Word is different from the beginning mentioned in Genesis 1:1. The beginning in Genesis 1:1 is the beginning of the universe, which happened in time and which can be reckoned by time.) Other verses that speak of the first eternity are John 17:24, Ephesians 1:4, and 1 Peter 1:20, which say, "Before the foundation of the world"; Ephesians 3:11, which speaks of "the eternal purpose" or "the purpose of the ages"; 2 Timothy 1:9 and Titus 1:2, which say, "Before the times of the ages"; and Romans 16:25, which says, "In the times of the ages." All of these verses cover the first eternity, the eternity that is without a beginning.

The Second Eternity

Isaiah 66:22 says, "The new heavens / And new earth... / Remain." Revelation 21:1 also speaks of the new heaven and new earth, and Revelation 22:5 speaks of "forever and ever." These verses tell us about the second eternity, which is the eternity without an ending and which is also beyond time.

The first eternity and the second eternity are joined in heaven; they are connected and span from eternity past to eternity future with no time element involved. We cannot say when eternity begins and when it ends. But at a certain point God created the universe. Time began from the foundation of the world, and thereafter, events can be reckoned in terms of time. From earth's point of view, eternity can be divided into two parts, with the portion of time that began from the foundation of the world linking the two parts of eternity. The eternity which existed before the foundation of the world was the first eternity, the eternity without a beginning, and the eternity which exists after the end of time is the second eternity, the eternity without an ending.

WHAT GOD'S ETERNAL WILL IS

With this understanding of eternity, we can consider God's eternal will. According to Ephesians 3:11, God has an eternal purpose, that is, an eternal will. In Greek the word *purpose* has the same root as the word *purposed* in Romans 1:13. God has an eternal will. This means that God made a decision in the first eternity. According to Ephesians 1:9, God's decision is according to His good pleasure; it is purposed in Himself; and it is for the purpose of making known to us the mystery of His will. In Greek the words *good pleasure* mean "joy" or "delight." Since God has a *delight,* He purposed a *will.* Since God has a *will,* He made a *plan.* Based on His plan, God has a *mystery* to fulfill this plan.

God's will is something that is hidden in God's heart, but His plan is something that is manifested to others. God's plan is God's center, which is also God's goal. God's eternal plan spans from eternity to eternity; it begins with His purpose and will in the first eternity and ends with its full consummation in the second eternity.

GOD'S PERFECT WILL AND PERMISSIVE WILL

God has two kinds of will. One is His perfect will, and the other is His permissive will. God's perfect will is His ordained will; it exists from eternity to eternity and is executed in heaven without any hindrance. God's permissive will originates from God's foreknowledge and is based on God's perfect will; it passes through the world and eventually ends up in eternity.

BEFORE THE FOUNDATION OF THE WORLD AND FROM THE FOUNDATION OF THE WORLD

God's Plan Being before the Foundation of the World

God's plan was made before the foundation of the world. What kind of plan did God make before the foundation of the world? The first thing God purposed before the foundation of the world was to love the Son. John 17:24 tells us that the Father loved the Son "before the foundation of the world." The second thing that God purposed before the foundation of the world was to foreordain His Son to be the Christ. First Peter 1:20 says that "before the foundation of the world" God foreordained the Son to be the Christ. However, Ephesians 1:4-5 also tells us that God "chose us" in Christ and predestinated us "unto sonship" before the foundation of the world. (He chose men, but He predestinated them unto sonship.) Not only did God foreordain the Son to be the Christ, He also chose us in Christ and predestinated us unto sonship. Second Timothy 1:9 says that God gave us grace "before the times of the ages." Titus 1:2 says that God promised us eternal life "before the times of the ages." He promised that we would participate in His life. These two verses tell us that in order to receive the sonship, God predestinated us unto grace and life. All of these things were purposed by God before the foundation of the world.

The Fulfillment of God's Plan Being from the Foundation of the World

God's plan was purposed *before* the foundation of the world, but the fulfillment of His plan is realized *from* the foundation of the world. God accomplishes His plan through time. How does God accomplish His plan? Revelation 13:8 tells us that the Lord was slain "from the foundation of the world." Moreover, our names are written in the book of life from the foundation of the world. Hebrews 4:3 says that "the works of creation were completed from the foundation of the world." Matthew 25:34 speaks of "the kingdom prepared...from the foundation of the world." It is within the span of time that God created all things and accomplished redemption through Christ, writing the names of the redeemed ones into the book of life, giving them eternal life, and through this, preparing His kingdom.

God's eternal will was purposed in the first eternity, that is, before the foundation of the world. This is God's perfect will. Although the eternal plan of God was purposed before the foundation of the world, it is accomplished from the foundation of the world by passing through the world. This is God's permissive will. God's eternal plan will be fulfilled in the second eternity.

Chapter Two

THE PRAYER THAT EXPRESSES GOD'S WILL

Scripture Reading: Matt. 6:9-13

WHAT IS PRAYER?

The Bible shows us what prayer is. First, God has a need; He has a purpose. Second, He puts this purpose within man through the Holy Spirit so that man feels this need as well. Third, man responds by uttering this purpose back to God through prayer. Fourth, God does His work and accomplishes this purpose. This is the meaning of prayer.

Let us read a few passages. Matthew 9:36 through 10:1 says, "And seeing the crowds, He was moved with compassion for them, because they were harassed and cast away like sheep not having a shepherd. Then He said to His disciples, The harvest is great, but the workers few; therefore beseech the Lord of the harvest that He would thrust out workers into His harvest. And He called His twelve disciples to Him and gave them authority over unclean spirits, so that they would cast them out and heal every disease and every sickness." According to this passage, (1) God is moved with compassion to save, (2) He wants man to pray, (3) man prays, and (4) God sends men to work and to save.

Ezekiel 36:37 says, "Thus saith the Lord God; I will yet for this be inquired of by the house of Israel, to do it for them; I will increase them with men like a flock." According to this verse, (1) God will increase Israel with men, (2) God wants men to pray for this matter, (3) men pray for this matter, and (4) God accomplishes it.

Isaiah 62:6-7 says, "Upon your walls, O Jerusalem, / I have appointed watchmen; / All day and all night / They will never keep silent. / You who remind Jehovah, / Do not be dumb; / And do not give Him quiet / Until He establishes / And until He makes Jerusalem / A praise in the earth." According to this verse, (1) God wants Jerusalem to become a praise in the earth, (2) He has appointed watchmen, (3) the watchmen pray, and (4) God fulfills their desire.

From these passages we see that all proper prayers issue from God's heart and express God's desire. Prayer implies that God has a desire. He wants to fulfill such a desire, yet He does not want to do it directly; He wants man to cooperate with Him on earth. For this reason He unveils His desire to man and charges man to pray. Only after man prays will He fulfill His desire. This is the meaning of prayer.

THE SIGNIFICANCE OF MATTHEW 6:9-13

The prayer the Lord taught the disciples in Matthew 6 touches God's will. God's eternal will is expressed through it. From this prayer, we can see God's heart's desire. We can also see what He wants to accomplish and how it is being accomplished.

THE SECTIONS OF MATTHEW 6:9-13

We can divide Matthew 6:9-13 into three sections. Verses 9 through 10 form the first section. Verse 11 to the end of the first sentence of verse 13 forms the second section. The second sentence of verse 13 to the end of the verse forms the third section. The first section is related to God, the second section is related to man, and the third section again relates to God and points out the underlying basis.

EXPOSITION OF MATTHEW 6:9-13

Section One

Verse 9 says, "Our Father who is in the heavens." "Our" denotes something corporate. In this prayer the words *our*, *us*, and *we* are used nine times. Although one prays this prayer alone in a "private room" (v. 6), its tone is not individual but corporate. "Who is in the heavens" denotes that our prayers have to reach the Holy of Holies (Heb. 10:19). In order for our prayers to reach the Holy of Holies, we cannot trust in our feelings; we must trust in the precious blood of the Lord Jesus. Furthermore, we must come to the Father in faith (v. 22). "Father" denotes that we have a life relationship with God. We pray in this way because we stand as sons. Only when we stand in such a position can we fulfill God's heart's desire.

"Your Name Be Sanctified"

Following this there are three things that we have to ask for: "Your name be sanctified," "Your kingdom come," "Your will be done, as in heaven, so also on earth." First we ask, "Your name be sanctified." In the Bible, the words *sanctification, holiness,* and *separation* are the same word in Greek. It means to set apart a person or a thing unto God. Whether we set ourselves apart or are set apart by someone, being set apart means to be sanctified.

There are two aspects to our sanctification. The first is positional and objective. For example, *men* can be sanctified:

(1) Aaron and his sons. Exodus 28:41 says, "And shalt anoint them, and consecrate them, and sanctify them, that they may minister unto me in the priest's office." Here we have the sanctification of Aaron and his sons.

(2) The firstborn. Exodus 13:2 says, "Sanctify unto me all the firstborn, whatsoever openeth the womb among the children of Israel, both of man and of beast: it is mine." Here we have the sanctification of the firstborn of Israel.

(3) The saints. Acts 9:13 says, "Lord, I have heard from many concerning this man, how many evil things he has done to Your saints in Jerusalem." The term "saints" shows that the disciples are sanctified.

(4) The wife, the husband, and the children. First Corinthians 7:14 says, "For the unbelieving husband is sanctified by the wife, and the unbelieving wife is sanctified by the brother; otherwise your children are unclean, but now they are holy." Here the husband and the wife are sanctified.

The Bible also mentions *things* being sanctified.

(1) Food. Leviticus 21:8 says, "You shall sanctify him, for he offers the food of your God."

(2) Every creature of God. First Timothy 4:5 says, "For it [every creature of God] is sanctified through the word of God and intercession." The above verses show us that both food and every creature of God can be sanctified.

Furthermore, the Bible also mentions *places* being sanctified.

(1) Jerusalem. Matthew 4:5 uses the phrase *holy city*, showing that Jerusalem is sanctified.

(2) The temple. Matthew 23:17 refers to the temple being sanctified.

(3) The altar. Matthew 23:17 and 19 say, "The temple which sanctifies the gold...the altar which sanctifies the gift." This speaks first of the temple and altar being sanctified, and then of the gold and gift being sanctified through the sanctification of the temple and the altar.

The second aspect of sanctification is experiential and subjective. It is sanctifying God's name through one's life.

(1) The Lord Jesus. Matthew 4:10 says, "Then Jesus said to him, Go away, Satan! For it is written, You shall worship the Lord your God, and Him only shall you serve." God's name is sanctified before Satan through the Lord Jesus.

(2) Enosh. Genesis 4:26 says, "And to Seth, to him also there was born a son; and he called his name Enosh: then began men to call upon the name of the Lord." God's name was sanctified before men through Enosh.

(3) Abraham. Genesis 14:22 says, "And Abram said to the king of Sodom, I have lifted up mine hand unto the Lord, the most high God, the possessor of heaven and earth." God's name was sanctified before the king of Sodom through Abraham. He called God the most high God.

Genesis 21:32-33, "Thus they made a covenant at Beersheba: then Abimelech rose up, and Phichol the chief captain of his host, and they returned into the land of the Philistines. And Abraham planted a grove in Beer-sheba, and called there on the name of the Lord, the everlasting God." In verse 33 God's name was again sanctified through Abraham. He called God the everlasting God.

(4) Isaac. Genesis 26:28 says, "And they [Abimelech, his friend Ahuzzath, and Phichol the chief captain of his army]

THE PRAYER THAT EXPRESSES GOD'S WILL

said, We saw certainly that the Lord was with thee: and we said, Let there be now an oath betwixt us, even betwixt us and thee, and let us make a covenant with thee." God's name was sanctified before Abimelech through Isaac.

(5) Jacob. Genesis 30:27 says, "And Laban said unto him, I pray thee, if I have found favor in thine eyes, tarry: for I have learned by experience that the Lord hath blessed me for thy sake." God's name was sanctified before Laban through Jacob.

(6) Joseph. Genesis 39:9 says, "There is none greater in this house than I; neither hath he [Potiphar] kept back any thing from me but thee, because thou art his wife: how then can I do this great wickedness, and sin against God?" God's name was sanctified before Potiphar through Joseph.

(7) David. First Samuel 17:46 says, "This day will the Lord deliver thee into mine hand; and I will smite thee, and take thine head from thee; and I will give the carcasses of the host of the Philistines this day unto the fowls of the air, and to the wild beasts of the earth; that all the earth may know that there is a God in Israel." God's name was sanctified before Goliath through David.

(8) Samson. Judges 16:28 says, "And Samson called on Jehovah and said, O Lord Jehovah, remember me, I pray; and strengthen me, I pray, this one time only, O God, that I may be avenged of the Philistines at once for my two eyes." God's name was sanctified before the Philistines through Samson.

(9) Elijah. In 1 Kings 18:37 Elijah said, "Hear me, O Lord, hear me, that this people may know that thou art the Lord God, and that thou hast turned their heart back again." God's name was sanctified before the priests of Baal through Elijah.

(10) Paul. In Acts 27:22-23 Paul stood and said, "And now I advise you to cheer up, for there will be no loss of life among you, but only of the ship. For this very night an angel of the God whose I am and whom I serve stood by me." The Lord's name was sanctified before Paul's companions through Paul.

Hence, sanctifying God's name is making God's name distinct in the ear of the hearer from all other names who are not God, such as the devil (John 8:44), the stomach (Phil.

3:19), and idols (Isa. 36:19). Sanctifying God's name is to make His name distinct whenever it is mentioned.

"Your Kingdom Come"

God's goal is to rule over the universe. His desire is to have a kingdom. "Your kingdom come" shows God's goal and desire. God wants to see His kingdom come soon. Once His kingdom comes, Satan will be overturned (Matt. 12:28). In the age of the kingdom, the overcomers will share Christ's glory, and Satan will be cast into the abyss and suffer shame. This is God's goal and desire. God wants man to pray according to this goal and desire. The Lord wants men to pray for God's kingdom to come to earth, which means for God's rule to come to earth and for God to gain His kingdom on earth.

"Your Will Be Done, as in Heaven, so Also on Earth"

God's will is never hindered in heaven. His will is frustrated from being executed on earth because the earth has been corrupted by Satan. It has been usurped by God's enemy. However, when the kingdom comes, the earth will be completely recovered, and God's will and desire will be executed on the earth as it is in heaven. Satan will be bound in the abyss (Rev. 20:3; cf. Luke 8:31, Dan. 10:13) and will no longer be able to frustrate God's will. Today the Lord wants men to pray for this and to hasten the manifestation of His will.

Section Two

When a man stands on God's side to contend for His name, His kingdom, and His will, the enemy will attack him constantly. Everyone who makes a stand for God will come under the enemy's attack. This is why there is the need for protection. If there is no protection from God, we would fail. God protects us in four areas.

Food

"Give us today our daily bread." Without food, man cannot survive, and he cannot live for God's will. Man cannot give up ground to the enemy through the matter of food. It says, *"Our* daily bread." An individual may not be lacking in anything, but God wants the corporate "us" to be without want.

Forgiving Debt

"Forgive us our debts, as we also have forgiven our debtors." "Debts" here does not refer directly to the offenses we have committed against others. Our sins are forgiven through the Lord's blood, yet our debts are forgiven through our forgiving our debtors.

Not Brought into Temptation

"Do not bring us into temptation." We should not anticipate temptation; rather, we should ask God to not bring us into temptation.

Deliverance from the Evil One

"Deliver us from the evil one." This is an opposing prayer that deals with Satan.

Section Three

"For Yours is the kingdom and the power and the glory forever. Amen." This section mentions three things that are God's: the kingdom, the power, and the glory. All three things belong to God forever. Satan will eventually be removed. The word "forever" signifies that Satan can never prevail. "Amen" means "yes." It is like signing a signature; everything is sealed.

GOD NEEDS MAN'S PRAYER

God's Word repeatedly shows us that He wants man to pray. Isaiah 45:11 says, "Thus says Jehovah, / The Holy One of Israel and the One who formed him, / Ask Me about the things to come concerning My sons, / And concerning the work of My hands, command Me." Jeremiah 29:12 says, "Then you will call upon Me and come and pray to Me, and I will listen to you."

Many people do not want to pray. God even wonders why men do not intercede. Isaiah 59:16 says, "And He saw that there was no man, / And He was appalled that there was no intercessor. / Therefore His arm brought salvation to Him, / And His righteousness sustained Him."

CHAPTER THREE

WHAT IS GOD'S ETERNAL WILL?

Scripture Reading: Eph. 3:11; 1:9-10

The verses above show us that God has an eternal plan (Eph. 3:11). This plan is the mystery of His will (1:9). It is something unknown to man. God's eternal will is that all things in the heavens and on earth be headed up in Christ (v. 10). In other words, Christ is to be the Head over all things. When this happens, everything in the universe will express the Lord. This is God's eternal will.

THE MYSTERY OF GOD

God's mystery was kept in silence in the times of the ages (Rom. 16:25). This mystery was hidden in God's heart and was not revealed to anyone. In the past generations, God did not tell anyone the reason He created all things (Eph. 3:5a, 9).

THE REVELATION OF THE MYSTERY

However, this mystery has been manifested (Rom. 16:26). God revealed this mystery to Paul. He also revealed it to the holy apostles and prophets (Eph. 3:3-5), and He enlightens all concerning it (v. 9).

GOD'S MYSTERY BEING CHRIST

What is God's mystery? Colossians 2:2 says that God's mystery is Christ. Hence, the mystery of God is Christ. God's will is for Christ to be the centrality of all things and for all things to be subject to Christ so that He may be Head over all things. Colossians 3:11 says, "Christ is all and in all." Colossians 1:18 says, "That He Himself might have the first place in all things." Concerning this mystery Ephesians 3:6 says, "That in Christ Jesus the Gentiles are fellow heirs and fellow members of the Body and fellow partakers of the promise through the gospel." God is always working towards this goal. In the fullness of the times (1:10), He will head up all things in Christ, the things in the heavens and the things on the earth. (The word "times" in the original Greek means "ages.") This means that all things will be gathered together in one place and will be crowned with the name of Christ.

The book of Ephesians tells us what the Lord has obtained and will obtain from the time of His resurrection until the time of the new heaven and new earth. This is why it speaks of the Lord being the Head over all things in the heavens and on the earth; it does not speak of Him being the Head of all things under the earth, because by then there will no longer be anything under the earth. The book of Philippians tells us what He has obtained from the time of His resurrection until His second coming. This is why it says that in the name of Jesus every knee should bow, of those who are "in heaven and on earth and under the earth" (2:10). Today there are many things under the earth that are still unsettled.

CONCLUSION

God's goal is twofold: First, it is for all things to manifest Christ. In other words, it is for Christ to be Head over all things. Second, it is for man to be like Christ, to have His life and His glory. Today many believers on earth are lacking in Christ, and many things are manifesting Satan. But God will eventually reach His goal. One day, all things will manifest Christ. We have to pray that we will gain more Christ and manifest Him more so that God's will can be fulfilled soon.

Chapter Four

THE SON OF GOD AND THE CHRIST

The Bible reveals that the Lord is both the Son of God and the Christ. Since the Bible uses both titles when it addresses Him, there must be a distinction between these two titles. Today we want to see the meanings of these two titles.

THE LORD BEING THE SON OF GOD

Concerning the Lord as the Son of God, we have the angel in Luke 1:35 who spoke this title to Mary. Peter received revelation from the Father and knew the Lord as the Son of God in Matthew 16:16. According to Romans 1:4, the Lord was designated the Son of God out of resurrection. According to John 20:31, a man is saved and receives God's life when he believes in the Son of God.

THE LORD BEING THE CHRIST

Concerning the Lord as the Christ, we have the angels in Luke 2:11 who declared that He is the Christ to the shepherds. Peter received revelation from the Father and knew Him as the Christ in Matthew 16:16. According to Acts 2:36, the Lord was made Christ after His resurrection. According to John 20:31, a man is saved through believing that Jesus is the Christ.

We can clarify this by the following chart:

The Lord Being the Son of God	The Lord Being the Christ
1. Spoken by the angel to Mary (Luke 1:35)	Spoken by the angels to the shepherds (Luke 2:11)
2. Received by Peter as revelation from the Father (Matt. 16:16)	Received by Peter as revelation from the Father (Matt. 16:16)

3. Designated out of resurrection (Rom. 1:4)   Appointed by God after resurrection (Acts 2:36)
4. Man's being saved by believing it (John 20:31)   Man's being saved by believing it (John 20:31)

THE MEANING OF THE SON AND THE MEANING OF THE CHRIST

The Lord is the Son of God as well as the Christ of God. The Son and Christ each signify different things. The Lord being the Son of God speaks of His divinity; it indicates that He is God. His title as the Son also denotes that He is equal with God and shares the same glory as God. Furthermore, the Son of God is God from eternity to eternity. The Lord being the Christ speaks of Him being the Executor of God's plan. When the Son took up God's plan, He became the Anointed One—Christ. He did not become Christ until He was anointed. When He took up God's plan, He became the Christ. We can clarify the meaning of the Son and Christ by another chart:

The Son

1. The Son having divinity, being God
2. The Son being equal with the Father and sharing the same glory as the Father
3. The Son being God from eternity to eternity

Christ

Christ being the Executor of God's plan

After taking up God's plan, the Son becoming the Anointed One—Christ

The Son becoming Christ after the time of His anointing

MAN SHARING A PART IN GOD'S PLAN

Ephesians 1:11 says, "In whom also we were designated as an inheritance, having been predestinated according to the purpose of the One who works all things according to the counsel of His will." The word "counsel" can also be translated as "plan." In God's plan we have become portions of "Christ." Hence, all of us together become the Christ. We become the Christ by being in Christ. First Corinthians 12:12 says, "For even as the body is one and has many members, yet all the members of the body, being many, are one body, so also is the Christ." This Christ is the corporate Christ, who is composed of the Head and the Body. Hence, we are the Christ in the big corporate Christ, and we have all become a part of Christ. Since God's plan is in Christ, we have become a part of God's plan as well.

THE ACCOMPLISHMENT OF GOD'S PLAN

God accomplishes His plan in two steps. First, we become subject to Christ and are headed up by Him (Eph. 4:15). Then all things become subject to Him and are headed up under Him (1:10). God's plan has to do with the whole universe. He heads up all things under the headship of Christ. But God does not carry out this work directly; He does it first in the church. He brings the church, which is Christ's Body, under the authority of Christ's headship. Then He brings the whole universe under the headship of Christ.

CHAPTER FIVE

THE REBELLION OF THE ANGELS

God created the angels with a free will, and God also created man with a free will. If the angels and man had been created without a free will, the Son would not be able to gain any glory, because anything which is dead has no meaning. If the angels and man, who were endowed with a free will, had allowed the Son to be the Head, the Son would have gained the glory. Yet the angels rebelled, man fell, and God's eternal plan was frustrated. God's original intention was to express the glory of Christ through all things and particularly through man. Because of the angels' rebellion and man's fall, God's plan was frustrated.

THE LORD'S RELATIONSHIP WITH THE ANGELS AND WITH MAN

According to God's ordination, the Lord took on the form of an angel before His incarnation, and He took on the form of a man after incarnation. In the Old Testament He was the Messenger of God (Gen. 22:11-12). In the New Testament He was made in the likeness of men (Phil. 2:7). The Lord took on the form of an angel temporarily. He took on the form of an angel for the purpose of revealing Himself to man. However, the Lord has also taken on the form of a man eternally. In the New Testament the Lord not only took on the form of a man but also became a man. Hence, the Lord's relationship with man is much more intimate than His relationship with the angels. Hebrews 2:16 says that God did not give help to the angels but to man. In God's plan the Son is joined with man, not with angels. Perhaps the angels are quite aware of this fact.

THE ORIGIN OF SATAN
Ezekiel 28:11-19

Revelation 12:4 tells us that when Satan rebelled against God, one third of the angels went with him and joined his rebellion. The word *Satan* in Greek means "the opposer." How did Satan become Satan? How did he rebel against God? What is the history of his rebellion? We can find the facts about Satan in Ezekiel 28:11-19 and in Isaiah 14:12-20. These passages show us how he was created, his original position before God, his beauty, his latter rebellion, and his ultimate fate.

Ezekiel 25 uses seventeen verses to describe the destruction of four kingdoms—Ammon, Moab, Edom, and Philistia. Between verses 26:1 and 28:19, there are seventy-six verses that describe one kingdom—Tyre. This is because the king of Tyre in 28:12 is a type of Satan. Therefore, the Bible places special emphasis on this kingdom and its king. All the adjectives used in verse 28:12 are superlative in nature. "Thou sealest up the sum, full of wisdom, and perfect in beauty." He was "full of wisdom." This wisdom was probably used originally to understand God's will. Therefore, Satan had the function of a prophet before his fall.

Verse 13 says, "Thou hast been in Eden the garden of God; every precious stone was thy covering, the sardius, topaz, and the diamond, the beryl, the onyx, and the jasper, the sapphire, the emerald, and the carbuncle, and gold." The Eden referred to here is different from the Eden spoken of in Genesis 2:8. This Eden denotes God's dwelling place in heaven. The precious stones denote God's light, and gold signifies God's glory; Satan had both. In comparing the precious stones that covered him and the stones that covered Aaron, we see that God had probably appointed him to be a priest (cf. Exo. 25:7; 28:9-14).

Ezekiel 28:13 continues, "The workmanship of thy tabrets and of thy pipes was prepared in thee in the day that thou wast created." Pipes require breath to produce sound. Hence, they signify life. Tabrets move the heart and express love. The tabrets and pipes signify God's delight. Musical instruments are always linked to the kings (1 Sam. 16:23; Isa. 14:11). This shows that he was a king. These three things reveal that Satan functioned as a prophet, priest, and king at the same time.

"Prepared in thee in the day that thou wast created" means that he belonged to the previous world, distinguishing him from the prince of Tyre in verse 2.

Verse 14 says, "Thou art the anointed cherub that covereth." The word "anointed" means that he was separated for God's commission. "Covereth" refers to the covering of the ark, the place where God's righteousness (signified by the blood) and God's glory (signified by God's appearance) are found. The cherub's duty is to lead men to worship the Lord (Rev. 4:9-10; 5:11-14). He was the one commissioned by God to lead the created hosts to worship God's righteousness and glory. This again shows his priesthood.

Verse 14 continues, "I have set thee so: thou wast upon the holy mountain of God." In the Bible mountains signify an administrative center. The great mountain in Daniel 2:35 typifies God's kingdom. The mountains in Revelation refer to God's administration centers. In this verse we are told that Satan was in the seat of God's administration and ruled over all things of that world.

"Thou hast walked up and down in the midst of the stones of fire." The stones of fire refer to God's light. This shows that he had intimate fellowship with God. According to Ezekiel 1:26, the cherubim are positioned under God's throne. This is confirmed by the picture in Exodus 24:10 and 17. This means that he was very close to God.

Ezekiel 28:15 says, "Thou wast perfect in thy ways from the day that thou wast created." Everything that God creates is perfect. Verse 15 continues, "Till iniquity was found in thee." The word "till" indicates a long period of time. God did not create a Satan; He created a cherub. After God's created cherub fell, he became Satan. The iniquity he committed brought sin into the universe.

Verse 16 says, "By the multitude of thy merchandise they have filled the midst of thee with violence, and thou hast sinned." Mr. Pember said that the word "merchandise" can be translated as "slander." The word *devil* in the original language means "the accuser" (Rev. 12:10). Satan's way of merchandising is to bribe men's hearts with little gifts and favors, as Absalom did.

"Therefore I will cast thee as profane out of the mountain of God." The word "profane" can also be translated "overstepping." It means going beyond one's rightful place. As a result God cast him out and stripped him of his rule.

The phrase "O covering cherub" reminded him of his name. "And I will destroy thee, O covering Cherub, from the midst of the stones of fire." This means that the fellowship was broken. But this does not mean that Satan could no longer go to God; it merely means that spiritual fellowship was terminated. Being cast out from the holy mountain denotes being stripped of his administrative post and the fact that he could no longer rule the universe. Being destroyed from the midst of the stones of fire refers to being stripped of the spiritual fellowship and the fact that he could no longer come near to God.

Verse 17 says, "Thine heart was lifted up because of thy beauty, thou hast corrupted thy wisdom by reason of thy brightness: I will cast thee to the ground." He became proud because of his beauty, and he overstepped his boundary. He also corrupted his wisdom by reason of his brightness. As a result he was cast to the ground. Originally his sphere was the universe. Now it is limited to the earth.

Verse 17 continues, "I will lay thee before kings, that they may behold thee." These kings were the angels who ruled the world together with Satan. But only one-third followed him. Those angels who did not follow him still rule the universe, and they are the kings referred to in this verse. (Psalm 82 shows us that there are many rulers in the universe.)

Ezekiel 28:18 says, "Thou hast defiled thy sanctuaries by the multitude of thine iniquities, by the iniquity of thy traffic; therefore will I bring forth a fire from the midst of thee, it shall devour thee, and I will bring thee to ashes upon the earth in the sight of all them that behold thee." This is the punishment of fire. The first world was destroyed by fire.

Verse 19 says, "All they that know thee among the people shall be astonished at thee: thou shalt be a terror, and never shalt thou be any more." After this verse the description switches back to the prince of Tyre spoken of in verse 2.

Isaiah 14:12-20

Isaiah 14:12-20 also gives us some facts about Satan. Verses 12 through 14 describe his past, while verses 15 through 20 tell us his present condition.

Verse 12 says, "How you have fallen from heaven, / O Daystar, son of the dawn! / How you have been hewn down to earth, / You who made nations fall prostrate!" "Daystar" refers to the morning stars mentioned in Job 38:7. The phrase "son of the dawn" refers to the fact that he was the first one created in the whole universe.

Verses 13 and 14 say, "But you, you said in your heart: / I will ascend to heaven; / Above the stars of God / I will exalt my throne. / And I will sit upon the mount of assembly / On the sides of the north. / I will ascend above the heights of the clouds; / I will be like the Most High." He said "I will" five times. This was the cause of his fall. This was not just a matter of the heart but a matter of the will. The "heaven" in verse 13 is different from the "heaven" in verse 12. The "heaven" in verse 12 is in contrast to earth, whereas the "heaven" in verse 13 is above "the heights of the clouds." This is God's administrative center, the place where God conducts His business. Satan's goal is to be God. He was higher than all the archangels already (Jude 9), yet he was not satisfied with this. He wanted to be equal with God.

Genesis 1:1-2 speaks of God's judgment on the world at that time. When one-third of the angels rebelled with Satan, there was a change in the universe, and God executed great judgment upon it. Genesis 1:1 says, "In the beginning God created the heaven and the earth." Heaven includes not only heaven but also the angels. After God judged the rebellious Satan, the earth became without form and void, and darkness was upon the face of the deep.

The first world that God created was good (Job 38:7; Isa. 45:18), because God is not a God of confusion (1 Cor. 14:33).

Yet the earth became without form and void through God's judgment (Jer. 4:23-26). The Bible shows us that the earth is the center of the universe. In the future, everything will happen on the earth. We can say that the earth is the center stage of the universe.

GOD'S PERMISSIVE WILL

Due to Satan's rebellion, the earth has become marred with sin, and heaven is also tainted with sin. According to Leviticus 16:14-15, when the priests offered the sin offering for the propitiation of sin, they had to bring the blood into the Holy of Holies and sprinkle it before the propitiation cover. Hebrews 9:24-26 tells us that Christ has entered the tabernacle not made with hands, the heavenly tabernacle, and has offered up Himself as the sacrifice. According to Colossians 1:20, the extent of propitiation or redemption is not limited to the earth; it includes heaven as well. Even heaven itself needs to be redeemed. According to Isaiah 30:26, the sun is tainted with sin and will be healed and restored to its original state. Of course, the earth has suffered the greatest judgment from God. God's explicit will is seen in Ephesians 1:10, which is to head up all things in Christ, the things in the heavens and the things on the earth. His dealing with Satan through man is according to His permissive will.

Chapter Six

GOD'S PURPOSE IN CREATING MAN

Genesis 1:28 tells us that after God created man, He blessed him and told him to be "fruitful, and multiply, and replenish the earth, and subdue it: and have dominion" over all things. On the one hand, God wants to deal with death by life through man's multiplication, and on the other hand, God gave Adam the authority to have dominion. This position and authority once belonged to Satan, but now God has replaced him with man.

Genesis 2:15 says, "And the Lord God took the man, and put him into the garden of Eden to dress it and to keep it." This shows that there was decay and corruption. Hence, there is the need for man to recover the situation. From these two passages we see that God has a fourfold intention in creating man: (1) multiplying—dealing with death; (2) having dominion—dealing with insubordination; (3) keeping—dealing with attacks; and (4) dressing—dealing with corruption.

THE RELATIONSHIP BETWEEN GOD, MAN, AND SATAN

Moreover, Genesis 2 shows us two trees, the tree of life and the tree of the knowledge of good and evil (vv. 9, 16-17). The principle of the tree of life is dependence on God, and the principle of the tree of the knowledge of good and evil is independence and alienation from God. These are the acts of Satan. God's will is done in heaven, while Satan's will is carried out in the air. Man's independent right is exercised on earth. Now the question is which side man will stand on. Eating of the tree of life means to join oneself to God, whereas eating of the tree of the knowledge of good and evil means to join oneself to Satan.

PSALM 8

When we come to Psalm 8, we can once again see that God's desire is related to man; He wants man to reign for Him on earth. Hebrews 2:5-10 tells us the way the Lord fulfills Psalm 8, whereas 1 Corinthians 15:24-28 tells us the time the Lord fulfills it. Psalm 8 places special emphasis on the earth (vv. 1, 9). It also emphasizes the name and the kingdom. Three things in Psalm 8 match Matthew 6:9-10: (1) God's name being sanctified, (2) God's kingdom coming, and (3) God's will being done on earth. Psalm 8 does not concern the new heaven and new earth, because there will be no sea in the new heaven and new earth. Psalm 8 concerns the kingdom.

Verse 1 says, "O Jehovah our Lord, / How excellent is Your name / In all the earth, / You who have set Your splendor above the heavens!" This tells us that God's glory is set above the heavens.

Verse 2 says, "Out of the mouths of babes and sucklings / You have established strength / Because of Your adversaries, / To stop the enemy and the avenger." Babes are the youngest ones. As far as the duration of the universe is concerned, man is a babe and a suckling. God's intention is to deal with His enemy Satan through man. In Matthew 21:16, the Lord quotes this verse, saying, "You have perfected praise." This shows that there is a question of warfare. Here is spiritual warfare.

Psalm 8:3 says, "When I see Your heavens, the works of Your fingers, / The moon and the stars, which You have ordained." This psalm was written in the night and therefore does not mention the sun.

Verse 4 says, "What is man, that You remember him, / And the son of man, that You visit him?" We have to marvel at God's selection of man.

Verse 5 says, "You have made him somewhat lower than angels / And have crowned him with glory and honor." In His creation, God has made man a little lower than the angels. However, man's position before God is higher than that of the angels. God has made man a little lower than angels temporarily (Heb. 2:5-10) in order to crown him with glory and honor. This is God's goal. A crown is a sign of reigning. Crowning man with glory and honor means that man is placed in the highest position and is made to be like God.

Psalm 8:6-8 says, "For You have caused him to rule over the works of Your hands; / You have put all things under his feet: / All sheep and oxen, / As well as the beasts of the field, / The birds of heaven and the fish of the sea, / Whatever passes through the paths of the seas." God gave man the authority to have dominion over all things because He wants man to deal with the enemy. This is ordained by God at the foundation of the world and will be manifested in the age of the kingdom (Heb. 2:5-10).

HEBREWS 2:5-10

Hebrews 2:5-10 quotes Psalm 8; it is also an exposition of Psalm 8. Verse 5 says, "For it was not to angels that He subjected the coming inhabited earth." God has not given the coming inhabited earth, which is the millennium, to the angels but to man.

Verses 6 through 8 say, "For one has solemnly testified somewhere, saying, 'What is man, that You bring him to mind? Or the son of man, that You care for him? You have made Him a little inferior to the angels; You have crowned Him with glory and honor and have set Him over the works of Your hands; You have subjected all things under His feet.' For in subjecting all things to Him, He left nothing unsubject to Him. But now we do not yet see all things subjected to Him." This tells us that God has entrusted the millennium to man.

Verse 9 says, "But we see Jesus, who was made a little inferior to the angels because of the suffering of death, crowned with glory and honor, so that by the grace of God He might taste death on behalf of everything." This indicates that the man spoken of in Psalm 8:4-5 is the Lord Jesus. The first man Adam failed, but the second man Jesus succeeded! This verse says that He was a little lower than the angels. This refers to His humanity. He was a little lower than the angels so that He could die for man.

Hebrews 2:10 says, "For it was fitting for Him, for whom

are all things and through whom are all things, in leading many sons into glory, to make the Author of their salvation perfect through sufferings." "Through whom are all things" refers to the source, whereas "for whom are all things" refers to the consummation. Man cannot be the one through whom are all things, but he can be the one for whom are all things. Man is unable to have dominion over the universe because of Adam's failure, but the Lord has fulfilled God's will. He is leading many sons of God into glory. This is what God is after.

FIRST CORINTHIANS 15:24-28

First Corinthians 15:24-28 speaks of the same thing. Verse 24 says, "Then the end, when He delivers up the kingdom to His God and Father, once He has abolished all rule and all authority and power." This verse is divided into two parts: (1) destroying the enemy, and (2) delivering up the kingdom to God the Father. Verses 25 and 26 expand the first part, while verses 27 and 28 expand the second part. "The end" refers to the millennium. "Abolish" means to destroy forever. "The kingdom" also refers to the millennium.

Verse 25 says, "For He must reign until God puts all His enemies under His feet." The Lord will reign, and God will destroy all His enemies.

Verse 26 says, "Death, the last enemy, is being abolished." Death is the last thing to be destroyed. Death will be eliminated from the church before the millennium, but will be eliminated from the universe after the millennium. (During the millennium there will still be death according to Isaiah 65:20.) The Lord has judged death on the cross, and He will execute this judgment in the millennium.

Verse 27 says, "For He has subjected all things under His feet. But when He says that all things are subjected, it is evident that all things are except Him who has subjected all things to Him." God is not included.

Verse 28 says, "And when all things have been subjected to Him, then the Son Himself also will be subjected to Him who has subjected all things to Him, that God may be all in all." This verse is similar to Ephesians 1:10. God the Father has purposed the eternal will. God the Son has accomplished the Father's purpose, and God the Spirit has joined man to the Son.

CHAPTER SEVEN

THE FALL OF MAN

Scripture Reading: Gen. 3

As far as God's eternal will is concerned, His goal is centered on Christ, but as far as His permissive will is concerned, His goal is centered on man. According to God's eternal will, all of His plans are centered upon Christ. Because of Satan's rebellion, however, God has to use man to deal with His enemy. God has His eyes on man and He gains man so that He can deal with His enemy through man. This is God's permissive will.

After finishing His work on each of the six days of creation, with exception of the second day, God saw that "it was good." After He created the firmament on the second day, He did not say that it was good. This is because Satan is in the air (Eph. 6:12). Genesis 3 is filled with Satan's work; however, it does not mention him by name. It only mentions the serpent. (The word *serpent* in the original language means "the shining one," which indicates that it was beautiful and attractive.) The Bible uses the cursed serpent to symbolize Satan. This shows that Satan is always working behind the scene.

Let us read chapter three of Genesis. Verse 1 says, "Now the serpent was more subtle than any beast of the field which the Lord God had made. And he said unto the woman, Yea, hath God said, Ye shall not eat of every tree of the garden?" The serpent looked first for the woman, the weaker one, and tempted her when she was separated from the man. Eve did not stand on the position that she should have stood on and became susceptible to temptation. The serpent pretended to be dumb and asked questions in order to stir her up to reason.

Verses 2 and 3 say, "And the woman said unto the serpent, We may eat of the fruit of the trees of the garden: but of the fruit of the tree which is in the midst of the garden, God hath said, Ye shall not eat of it, neither shall ye touch it, lest ye die." Eve opened the door first; she brought up the tree of knowledge first.

Verses 4 and 5 say, "And the serpent said unto the woman, Ye shall not surely die: for God doth know that in the day ye eat thereof, then your eyes shall be opened, and ye shall be as gods, knowing good and evil." The serpent did two things. First, he lied about God, saying that God did not love them. Second, he told Eve that they would be like God if they ate of the tree of the knowledge of good and evil. In the beginning God forbade them to eat of the tree of the knowledge of good and evil because He wanted man to remain a man. Although they could become like God, they were not allowed to do it. But Satan told them that they could do it. This seemed to give Eve a new light and new revelation. Satan's goal is to induce man to leave his proper position.

Verse 6 says, "And when the woman saw that the tree was good for food, and that it was pleasant to the eyes, and a tree to be desired to make one wise, she took of the fruit thereof, and did eat, and gave also unto her husband with her; and he did eat." Both Adam and Eve ate the fruit of the tree of the knowledge of good and evil.

Verse 7 says, "And the eyes of them both were opened, and they knew that they were naked; and they sewed fig leaves together, and made themselves aprons." Two things happened at this point: (1) They acquired God's knowledge, and (2) they knew that they were sinners. Man acquired knowledge, yet at the same time he became a sinner. From this point on, there was no other destiny for man except death.

In verses 8 through 13, God only questioned man; He did not ask the serpent anything. On the surface man was beguiled by the serpent. In fact, however, God won the victory, and Satan was defeated, because Satan's fate became tied to man through this act. In Genesis 2:15 man could only guard the garden from attack, but he could not destroy Satan. After Satan gained man, Satan was bound and could no longer move freely. We can illustrate this by an example from a legal court. A culprit and his accomplice cannot be separated. Satan is the culprit, while man is the accomplice. Legally speaking the culprit and the accomplice must be together. Whatever punishment the culprit receives the accomplice will receive as well, and vice versa. Hence, Satan's fate was tied to man.

Genesis 3:14 says, "And the Lord God said unto the serpent, Because thou hast done this, thou art cursed above all cattle, and above every beast of the field; upon thy belly shalt thou go, and dust shalt thou eat all the days of thy life." This was a punishment for the serpent. The serpent became closer to the earth, and man became his food (because Adam was made of dust). He could only eat man and be joined to man. Hence, if God can deal with man, He will deal with the serpent as well, because the two have become one. Consequently, when Christ judged Adam on the cross, He judged Satan as well. Satan's victory has indeed become his loss. There is a difference between walking upon feet and walking upon the belly. The serpent walks upon his belly; he touches the earth and is bound by the earth. But man walks upon his feet, which is only a very small part of his body. Satan was bound to the earth and could only have man as his food. If God redeems man and the earth, Satan will be left with nothing.

Here we must remember three important things: (1) God's eternal will is for Christ to be the Head. (2) Satan rebelled against God, and God appointed man to stand against Satan. (3) Man fell. God wants to accomplish His eternal will, but He needs to solve two problems—Satan's rebellion and man's fall. First, He has to deal with the rebellious Satan. Second, He has to take care of man's fall. In the next chapter we will see how God dealt with these two problems.

CHAPTER EIGHT

THE WORK OF CHRIST

We have mentioned before that God's eternal plan is for Christ to be glorified and to be made the Head over all things. When Satan rebelled and man fell, God had to come in to deal with these two problems before He could accomplish His eternal plan. Originally God created man with the purpose of having man deal with the rebellious Satan and to displace his rule. But man was deceived and fell. Now God had to take care of two problems. What did He do? He dealt with these two problems through the Lord Jesus. Today we will consider the work of the Lord in God's plan: how He solved the problems that stood in the way of God's plan and how He accomplished God's plan. The Lord's work was carried out mainly on the cross. On the cross He dealt with sin and the sinner. He redeemed us from sin and removed us, the sinners. This is the negative side of the Lord's work. In addition, the Lord stood in the place of Adam, that is, in the place of man and opposed, withstood, and defeated Satan by exercising His will as a man and seized the power of authority back from Satan.

HIS BIRTH IN BETHLEHEM

Every incident in the Lord's life was connected to God's plan and related to the destruction of Satan. First, He was born in Bethlehem, taking on a body of blood and flesh (Heb. 2:14). This was not only for the purpose of having blood and shedding blood to forgive our sins, but also for the purpose of dealing with Satan. God wants the created man to deal with Satan. Satan could never touch the will of the man Jesus. In the second man Jesus, God gained what He could not gain in the first man Adam.

HIS TEMPTATION IN THE WILDERNESS

After the Lord was baptized by John in the Jordan, He rose up from the water and a voice from heaven said, "This is My Son, the Beloved" (Matt. 3:16-17). Then the Lord was led by the Holy Spirit into the wilderness and tempted by the devil (4:1-11). In the first temptation the devil said to Him, "If You are the Son of God..." (v. 3). Satan wanted Him to be the Son of God rather than a man. He wanted the Lord to leave His position as a man and take the position of the Son of God, that is, to be God. This was Satan's deception. Satan knew that once the Lord took the position of God, He would lose His position to deal with him. But the Lord saw through Satan's deception, and He answered saying, "Man shall not live..." (v. 4). It seems as if the Lord was saying, "I am here as a man, not as the Son of God. Although I am the Son of God, I am taking the position of a man." The first Adam, who was a man, wanted to be God and failed. The second Adam, who is God, was willing to stand in the position of a man and prevailed. Only *man* can accomplish God's eternal plan and only *man* can deal with Satan.

In the second temptation Satan seemed to be saying, "If You are a man after God's heart, You should be able to jump down from the wing of the temple. God will surely protect You." (There is no love in Satan's temptation. Wherever there is love, there is not temptation.) Temptation comes when a person does not understand God's will. When a person is ignorant, he will try anything. Satan tried to completely separate the Lord from God once He firmly stood in the position of a man. Yet the Lord would not tempt God. He knew that He was joined to God, and He did not doubt God. Hence, He did not take Satan's suggestion to tempt God by jumping down from the temple. In the temptations that the Lord encountered in the wilderness, He was tempted to give up his position as a man and He was tempted to doubt whether He was one with God.

In the third temptation the devil said, "If You will fall

down and worship me" (v. 9). Satan's goal is worship. Since the Lord represented all men, all men would have failed if He had worshipped Satan. But the Lord stood on God's side. He only worshipped God and served Him. He overcame Satan's temptations. In the garden of Eden man's will sided with Satan and brought in his utter failure. In the wilderness man's will sided with God and was one with God. As a result man completely overcame.

HIS CRUCIFIXION ON GOLGOTHA

The center of God is Christ, whereas the center of Christ is the cross. When the Lord became a man, He became a representative of all men and included all men. Because He included all men, all men suffered God's punishment when He was crucified on the cross and shed His blood (2 Cor. 5:14). He included all men. Hence, when He died on the cross, everyone in Adam died as well.

HIS VICTORY IN RESURRECTION

The Lord is the resurrection (John 11:25). Resurrection is that which overcomes death and that which cannot be defeated by death. Through death, the Lord destroyed the devil who has the might of death and released men from the slavery of death (Heb. 2:14-15). The Lord is the resurrection. Hence, death could not lay hold of Him, and Hades could not keep Him. The one who had the power of death lost his authority over Him. Colossians 2:15 says, "Stripping off the rulers and the authorities, He made a display of them openly, triumphing over them in it." The words "stripping off" mean that Satan could not lay hold of anything or keep anything. Originally, Satan's food was dust (which was man). But now that the Lord has died and resurrected, His life is the resurrection life, and the resurrection life has nothing to do with dust. Therefore, through the death of Christ, dust (that is, man) is buried, and the rulers and authorities are also buried. This is the reason that Satan hates baptism. Baptism signifies burial, and everything in Adam has been stripped off through the water of burial and is buried in the grave. Satan has no more food to eat. Those who have risen from the water of baptism are men in resurrection. They are no longer dust, and Satan no longer has any authority over them.

Through death the Lord Jesus destroyed the one who held the power of death. He stood in the position of a man and overcame Satan on behalf of man. He is the victorious One, and we whom He represents are also victorious. He has gained the victory, and we are enjoying His victory. In the Bible there are victories, and there are those who boast in victories. There is a difference between victory and boasting in victory. Victory is overcoming in the battlefield, while boasting in victory is singing the victory celebration after the battle has been won. Christ has won the victory, and we who are on His side only need to boast in His victory. This is like a school whose sports team has won the victory. All the students in the school rejoice and boast in the victory. The minute we boast in victory, we rejoice. This is what Psalm 23:5 means when it says, "You spread a table before me / In the presence of my adversaries." Christ has won the victory, and in Him we boast in His victory.

Both John 16:11 and Revelation 12:11 speak of the cross dealing with Satan. The Lord on the cross was a representation. In its representation, the world was also on the cross (Gal. 6:14), and the prince of the world was also on the cross. In God's eyes the whole world is one entity. Satan is the head of the world. When the Lord was lifted up on the cross, Satan was cast out (John 12:31-33). John 3:14 says, "And as Moses lifted up the serpent in the wilderness, so must the Son of Man be lifted up." The bronze serpent which Moses lifted up (bronze being a type of judgment) shows God's judgment. Not only did He judge men, He also judged Satan. After man sinned and fell, he became God's enemy. In John 8:44, the Lord says, "You are of your father the devil." When man followed the devil, he became the descendant of the serpent. Hence, when the Lord was crucified, the descendants of the serpent were included in His crucifixion. As the bronze serpent the Lord does not have the poison of the serpent. He suffered God's judgment as a representative of us, the descendants of the serpent. He bore man's sin, yet He Himself did not know sin (2 Cor. 5:21). The blood of the Lamb enables us to overcome Satan (Rev. 12:11), because the Lord as the bronze serpent has become a representative of the descendants of the serpent. When He was crucified on the cross, Satan was dealt with as well. Hence, the Lord has won the victory.

HIS EXALTATION IN ASCENSION

Ephesians 1:20-22 says, "Which He caused to operate in Christ in raising Him from the dead and seating Him at His right hand in the heavenlies, far above all rule and authority and power and lordship and every name that is named not only in this age but also in that which is to come; and He subjected all things under His feet and gave Him to be Head over all things to the church." These three verses mention the Lord's resurrection and ascension. Resurrection and ascension are equally important. God's will is in heaven, man's will is on earth, and Satan the enemy is in the air. When the Lord ascended, He transcended over all His enemies. Today the Lord occupies such an exalted position that the enemy cannot even touch Him. Ascension signifies a victorious stand, and ascension brings in a new position. Heaven is not part of the enemy's territory, and Satan cannot touch this realm at all. We who are now in Christ and in heaven are also beyond Satan's touch. Ephesians 1:20-22 tells us that the Lord is in heaven, while Ephesians 2:6 tells us that we are seated in the heavenlies with the Lord. The Lord ascended to heaven as a man. This means that now a man has ascended to God. He is a glorified man. He is the first Overcomer. He is the first Man before God. As a man He has transcended over everything.

Christ defeated the enemy through His birth, temptation, human living, crucifixion, resurrection, and ascension. He dealt with the enemy as a man and in the position of a man. Because of His victory, God's will in man is fulfilled. By becoming a man, Christ overcame the enemy and accomplished God's eternal purpose.

CHAPTER NINE

THE ORGANIZATION, GOAL, AND METHODS OF SATAN'S KINGDOM

Scripture Reading: Col. 1:13; Acts 26:18; 2 Cor. 2:11; Matt. 12:25-26

These few verses show us that Satan has a kingdom. They also show us that Satan has his authority and deceptions. Many believers fail because they are ignorant of the enemy's deceptions. Colossians 1:13 and Acts 26:18 clearly show that Satan has a kingdom and authority. When the Lord talks about a kingdom divided against itself in Matthew 12, He is talking about the kingdom of Satan. The Lord knows that Satan has a kingdom. Today we want to see the organization of Satan's kingdom, the goal of his kingdom, and the methods he employs to reach his goal.

THE ORGANIZATION OF SATAN'S KINGDOM

There are two sides to the organization of Satan's kingdom—the spiritual side and the physical side. He uses spiritual materials as well as physical materials to build up his kingdom. On the spiritual side, there are corrupted angels and unclean demons, that is, evil spirits. On the physical side, there is man.

Spiritual Materials

Satan Himself—Revelation 12:9

The Hebrew word for Satan is used thirty-five times in the Old Testament. Its Greek equivalent is used thirty-eight times in the New Testament. In the Bible, several names are associated with Satan:

(1) The dragon (Rev. 12:3-4, 9). The dragon is the one who deceives the whole world. He is referred to in 1 Thessalonians 3:5 as "the tempter." He has seven heads and ten horns and is very powerful.

(2) The serpent (Gen. 3:1-15). The serpent is most beguiling in seducing men to sin and become fallen.

(3) The devil (Rev. 12:9). The meaning of the word *devil* is "the accuser" or "the slanderer." He accuses us before God and slanders us before men.

(4) Satan (Rev. 12:9). The meaning of the word *Satan* is "the adversary." He is God's adversary, opposing and rebelling against God.

(5) Apollyon (Rev. 9:11). The meaning of the word *Apollyon* is "the destroyer." He is a cruel and treacherous enemy.

(6) Beelzebul (Matt. 12:24). The meaning of *Beelzebul* is "the lord of the dunghill." This means he nags and annoys.

The Corrupted Angels—
Matthew 25:41

Revelation 12:4 tells us that one-third of the angels fell and followed Satan when he rebelled against God. With them Satan organized a kingdom of darkness. The "world-rulers of this darkness" in Ephesians 6:12 and the "rulers and authorities" in Colossians 2:15 refer to them.

Psalm 82 also speaks concerning them. In verse 1 "the congregation of God" and "the gods" refer to these angels. They have been sent by Satan to rule over this world and to deal cruelly with men. In verses 1 through 4 God rebuked their unrighteousness and exhorted them. In verse 5 we are told that they did not take heed to His rebuke and exhortation. Verses 6 and 7 speak of God's judgment and punishment concerning them, and verse 8 is a prayer of the psalmist.

Daniel 10:13-21 mentions two princes, who are evil, ruling angels, that is, the rulers and authorities under Satan's hand. This passage of the Scriptures shows that behind every nation there is an evil angel sent from Satan, who manipulates its politics behind the scenes.

The Little Demons

There are countless numbers of demons. They are not in the air but on earth. They primarily attach themselves to men, pigs, or idols (Matt. 12:43-45; Luke 8:33; 1 Cor. 10:20). They like to lodge themselves in the human body. These demons were probably citizens of the former world. As proof: (1) They are different from the angels (Acts 23:9), (2) they are different from the spirits of the dead people (Job 7:9), and (3) they are spirits that have been separated from their bodies (Matt. 8:16; Luke 10:17, 20; Matt. 17:18; Mark 9:25). They are divided according to the nations of this world, and each one has his own territory, sphere, and boundaries. They are limited by regional boundaries (Luke 8:31).

Satan's kingdom is tightly organized, and its numerous messengers keep close surveillance on every move of man. This is why we have to cast out demons and withstand their activities when we pray. These demons are the creatures of the former world who became disembodied spirits (their bodies having been destroyed). When they possess man's body:

(1) Man becomes bent double and cannot stand erect at all (Luke 13:11).

(2) Man becomes dumb (Matt. 9:33).

(3) Man is driven to insanity (Matt. 8:28).

(4) Man worships idols (1 Cor. 10:20-21; Rev. 9:20; 2 Chron. 11:15; Lev. 17:7; Deut. 32:17).

More than one demon can possess a human body (Mark 16:9). But a demon can possess only one body. The evil angels are the rulers of this world, while the little demons are out to frustrate men, to torment men, to drive men to insanity, and to motivate men to worship idols. When demons attach themselves to idols, they seduce men to worship them and rob men of their worship of the true God.

Physical Materials

First John 5:19 says, "The whole world lies in the evil one." Satan is the prince of this world, and the whole world, including man, is under his domination. In order to deal with ordinary men, he only needs to release the little demons. But in order to deal with godly men who stand absolutely one with God, like Daniel, he has to call in the princes. (Of course, God also sends angels to protect these godly ones.)

THE GOAL OF SATAN'S KINGDOM

Satan's tightly organized kingdom and numerous messengers exist for the sole purpose of achieving his evil goal. Satan desires four things:

(1) In eternity he wanted to be the Most High (Isa. 14:14).

(2) In the garden of Eden he wanted to be like God (Gen. 3:5).

(3) In the wilderness he wanted to be worshipped (Luke 4:7).

(4) In the temple he will want to be God (2 Thes. 2:4).

Satan's consistent goal is to be God and to be worshipped as God. In order to achieve this, he has formed a tightly organized kingdom. He controls all the materials in it on the one hand, and he tries to build up his kingdom on earth on the other hand. He knows that God eventually will establish His kingdom on earth, and he has gone a step ahead of God to establish his own. Genesis 6 reveals how Satan corrupted the men God had created. In Genesis 11, Satan instigated men to corporately rebel against God by building the tower of Babel to make a name for themselves. In Egypt Satan used Pharaoh to persecute the Israelites (Exo. 1:8-22). The great image in Daniel 2:31-43 signifies the earthly kingdoms which are established by Satan himself. These kingdoms up- lift men, rebel against God, and withstand God's kingdom (which at that time was Israel).

THE METHODS OF SATAN'S KINGDOM

His Work in the World

(1) Blinding men's thoughts (2 Cor. 4:4).

(2) Stealing men's worship (Rev. 13:12).

(3) Snatching away God's word which men have heard, so that men forget what they have heard (Matt. 13:19).

(4) Bringing in counterfeits—religion and morality (1 Tim. 4:1-3).

Satan knows that God hates the flesh. Therefore, he pretends to hate it by instigating men to be vegetarians and to abstain from marriage. He also wins men's hearts by promoting culture and science, creating confusion to convince men of their impotence, and creating false peace to cover up his darkness.

His Work in the Church

(1) Persecutions, threats (Rev. 2:10; Acts 5:28).

(2) Attacks on the body (2 Cor. 12:7).

(3) Counterfeits, slanders, and lies (2 Cor. 11:13-15; Rev. 2:9; 3:9).

(4) Filling men's hearts and causing men to become covetous (Acts 5:3). This shows us that it is difficult to separate Satan from money.

We have to pay attention to Satan's works. Concerning everything that happens to us, we should not ask what it is but where it is coming from. It is not a matter of good or bad but a matter of the source. Everything that Satan does is with a view to increase his power, kingdom, and authority. He is doing everything he can to oppose God. He exhausts all of his tactics and employs all of his messengers to do just one thing—win men over. The kind of people he is most afraid of are those who do God's will. Today God's goal is to gain men who will destroy all the works of Satan. Satan's goal is to win men over to oppose God's will. This is a warfare between two thrones. God wants men to destroy Satan's will, while Satan wants men to destroy God's will. May the Lord clearly show us Satan's kingdom, organization, and evil plots. May God cause us to be those who only love His will so that we can deal with Satan, His adversary.

CHAPTER TEN

THE POSITION AND RESPONSIBILITY OF THE CHURCH

Scripture Reading: Eph. 1:20-23

THE CHURCH BEING THE CONTINUATION OF CHRIST'S POSITION AND WORK

We have seen the work of the Lord as well as the kingdom and the evil intention of Satan. Now we come to the position and responsibility of the church. In the eyes of God the church occupies a very important place. Its position is that of being joined to Christ, and its responsibility is to continue the warfare that Christ fought on earth. Christ the Head has ascended, but His Body is still on earth. The church, as the Body of Christ, is His propagation, continuing His stand and work to fight against God's enemy.

Ephesians 1:20-23 shows us that the power which operated in Christ not only raised Him from the dead, but caused Him to ascend to the heavens. This resurrection power is the power of ascension. Through His resurrection the church received its life, and through His ascension the church assumed its position of authority and inherited the kingdom. In this way, He brought heaven to earth, and His will can be done on earth, as in the heavens. Christ ascended to the heavens and received the heavenly authority; now He is able to bring heaven to earth. Resurrection alone is not enough; there must also be ascension. When we stand in the heavenly position, we transcend all things. When the Lord ascended to the heavens, He transcended all the powers of the enemy, and God subjected all things under His feet. (Of course, this is not fully manifested at the present time.)

Christ ascended and became "Head over all things to the church" (Eph. 1:22). Verse 23 clearly shows that the church and Christ are inseparable. The church is filled with Christ; it is the fullness of Christ, the overflow of Christ. God's desire is to gain a corporate man. The church, which is formed of individual saints who are put into Christ, is the corporate Christ; it is the combination of all the small portions of Christ in the saints. As the Body of Christ, the church is the continuation of Christ. Everything that belongs to Christ belongs to the church. The position that Christ attained is the position that the church has attained. The works that Christ accomplished are sustained and perpetuated through the church.

THE CHURCH STANDING BETWEEN
THE CROSS AND THE KINGDOM

The cross of Christ produced the church, and the church brings in the kingdom. Hence, the church stands between the cross and the kingdom. The present age is the time for the church to practically realize the victory of Christ. The Head has overcome; now the Body must also overcome. The Lord destroyed the devil on the cross and produced the church with resurrection life. Today God is establishing His kingdom on earth through His church. The church must continue the victorious work that Christ has carried out against Satan. It is responsible for bringing heaven's will down to earth and for carrying it out on earth.

THE CHURCH CONTINUING
CHRIST'S BATTLE ON EARTH

In John 12—16 Satan is spoken of as the ruler of this world three times (12:31; 14:30; 16:11). Presently, he is the ruler of this world, and the nations of this world are his domain. In the millennium, he will be bound and cast into the abyss. Before that time, the church is on the earth to curb the activities of Satan. The prayer of the church is the most effective means of curbing Satan. The church is a miniature of the kingdom. Any place that manifests God's authority is a place where the kingdom is realized (Matt. 12:28). It is our responsibility to put a halt to Satan's will. Wherever the church is, Satan's authority will retreat. The church is on the earth to perpetuate and manifest Christ's victorious stand over Satan.

THE CHURCH CARRYING OUT GOD'S WILL ON EARTH

Subduing the Rulers and Authorities

The church has a great responsibility on the earth today. On the negative side, the church has to subdue the power of darkness and continue the warfare that Christ waged against Satan. On the positive side, the church brings God's will to earth. Wherever we are, we should stand firm. When we read the daily news, we can find where the enemy is working, and we should render proper, opposing prayers. Second Corinthians 10:4 says, "For the weapons of our warfare are not fleshly but powerful before God for the overthrowing of strongholds." Ephesians 6:12 says, "For our wrestling is not against blood and flesh but against the rulers, against the authorities, against the world-rulers of this darkness, against the spiritual forces of evil in the heavenlies." Our prayer must be powerful before God in order to oppose the power of darkness. Before we can reign in the future, we have to learn to rule over everything today. We rule over the thrones on earth by the throne in heaven. Believers fail because they have not exercised their authority; they have not prayed to reign over the political events. As soon as we see the devil's power or work, we should exercise our authority to pray. If there were no Christians on earth today, the world would be like hell. We have to learn to exercise the overcoming authority of Christ to rule over the power of darkness.

Preaching the Gospel

Everyone in this world is a captive of Satan. But God wants the Christians to recapture the captives through the gospel and win them back to God's side. When God wins one more person, Satan has one less person. First Timothy 2:4 says, "Who desires all men to be saved and to come to the full knowledge of the truth." This shows that the gospel is part of

God's will. God delivers men with the purpose of saving them to the extent that God's authority can be fully manifested through them. God wants us to preach the gospel and through it to carry out His will. Those who do not open their mouths and do not testify for God have failed to uphold God's will.

Casting out Demons

Every believer should be able to cast out demons; this act also carries out God's will. When we cast out the demons by the Spirit of God, the kingdom of God has come upon us (Matt. 12:28).

Overturning Anything Not Found in Heaven

We have to overturn anything on earth that is not found in heaven. In heaven there is no lawlessness, sickness, weakness, or hunger because God's will is done in the heavens. If these things come to us through God's permission, they will go away after awhile (Matt. 10:29; Job 38:8-11; Jer. 5:22). But if they are from Satan, they will not go away, even after months and years. We have to differentiate between the things that God has allowed to come upon us and the things that Satan has set to ensnare us. We have to reject anything that comes to us without God's permission. The earth should have only that which is found in heaven. Whatever heaven does not have should not be found on the earth. This is the church's responsibility on the earth.

Absolutely Obeying God's Will

The church must obey God's will absolutely. His will must be done in man before it can be done on earth. Nothing can replace God's will, not even sacrifice, zeal, or work. It is not a matter of good or evil but a matter of God's will. If a work cannot be linked to God's will and cannot inflict loss to the gates of Hades, it is useless. God brings us through many trials because He wants His will to be done, not because He is cruel. God tests us again and again to see what and who we are living for.

Not Having Private Associations

In the casting out of the demon in Acts 19:13-16, we see that the enemy fears only those who do not associate with him in private. He recognizes those who refuse to associate with him. In the kingdom of the demons, a well-recognized name carries much weight. The devil knows and fears men such as Paul, whose names are well-recognized and who are absolutely for God. Some Christians secretly want to associate themselves with the devil. The devil only laughs at such ones because they are not absolute for God's will. They can never shake the gates of Hades. Only those who are absolute and who do not associate themselves with the devil privately will bring God's will to earth.

Praying

Genuine prayer is a joint labor with God to bring His kingdom to the earth and to carry out His will on earth. Hence, prayer is nothing less than a spiritual battle (2 Cor. 10:2, 4; Matt. 6:10; Eph. 6:12). Prayer overturns the power of darkness and opens the way for God's will to be executed on earth.

Not Belonging to the World

We are above the world; we do not belong to this world (John 17:16). Through the cross God delivered us out of this world unto Himself and His will (Gal. 6:14). We should not belong to this world, and we should not return to the reign of Satan. Once we are not of this world, Satan will not have any ground in us. When we are not of this world, we will be free from Satan's authority, and we will be delivered from His reign and kingdom. In this way, God's will can be carried out on earth.

May God execute His will and accomplish His purpose through the church. The church's responsibility on the earth today is to perpetuate Christ's victory on the earth and to bring in God's kingdom. When the church is faithful to its position and responsibility, God's eternal purpose will be accomplished.